First published in Japan in 2003 by Child Honsha Co., Ltd. under the title *999-hiki no kyôdai no ohikkoshi*.
First published in the United States, Great Britain, Canada, and Australia in 2011
by North-South Books Inc., an imprint of NordSüd Verlag AG, CH-8005 Zürich, Switzerland.
English translation by Child Honsha Co., Ltd. and Japan Foreign-Rights Centre. Edited by Susan Pearson.
Distributed in the United States by North-South Books Inc., New York 10016.

Library of Congress Cataloging-in-Publication Data is available.
Printed in China by Leo Paper Products Ltd., Heshan, Guangdong, November 2011.
ISBN: 978-0-7358-4013-3 (trade edition)

3 5 7 9 · 10 8 6 4 2

www.northsouth.com

®
FSC
www.fsc.org
MIX
Paper from
responsible sources
FSC® C020056

999 TADPOLES

by Ken Kimura

illustrated by

Yasunari Murakami

NorthSouth
New York / London

One warm spring day, 999 tadpoles were born. Although they were tiny, they were full of energy. Mother and Father Frog were very proud.

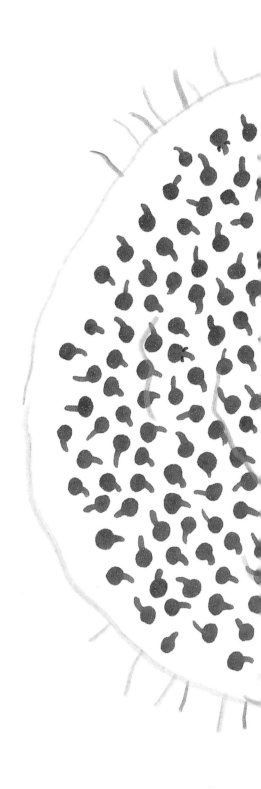

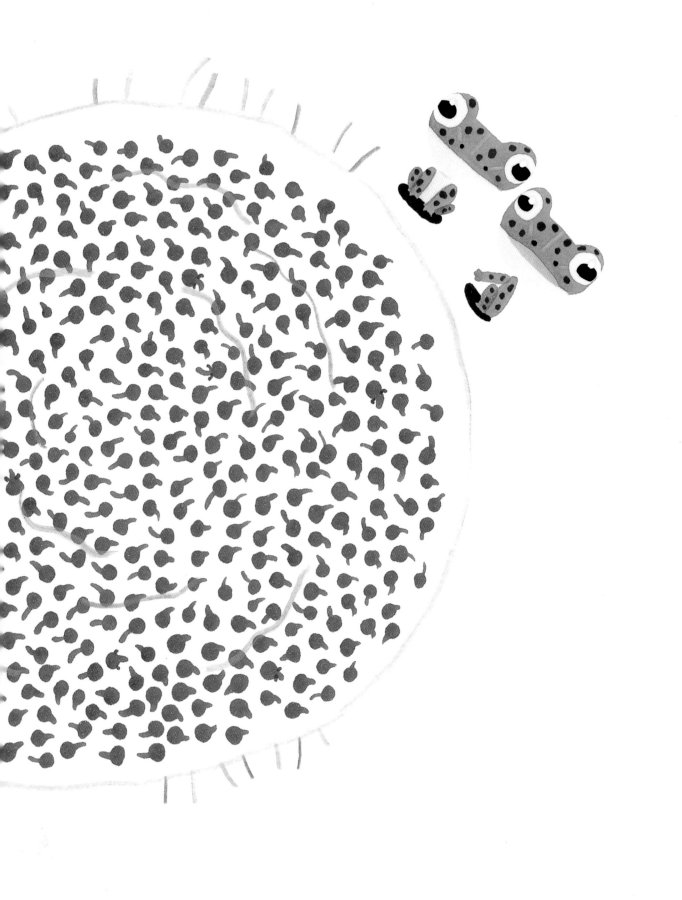

The 999 tadpoles grew and grew and grew, until one day they grew into frogs. Now the pond was too small for them.

"We can't move!" one called.

"We can't breathe!" called another.

"Don't push!" called a third.

"We have a situation here," said Father.

"We'll have to move," said Mother.

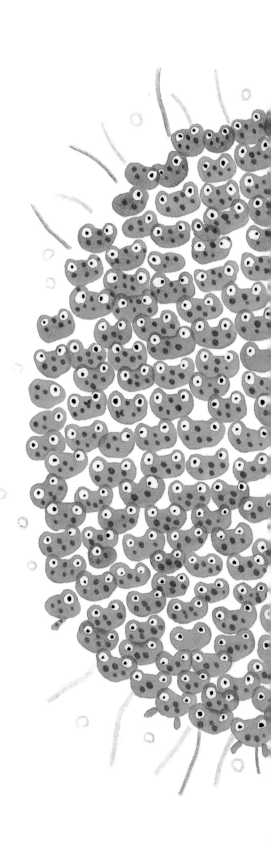

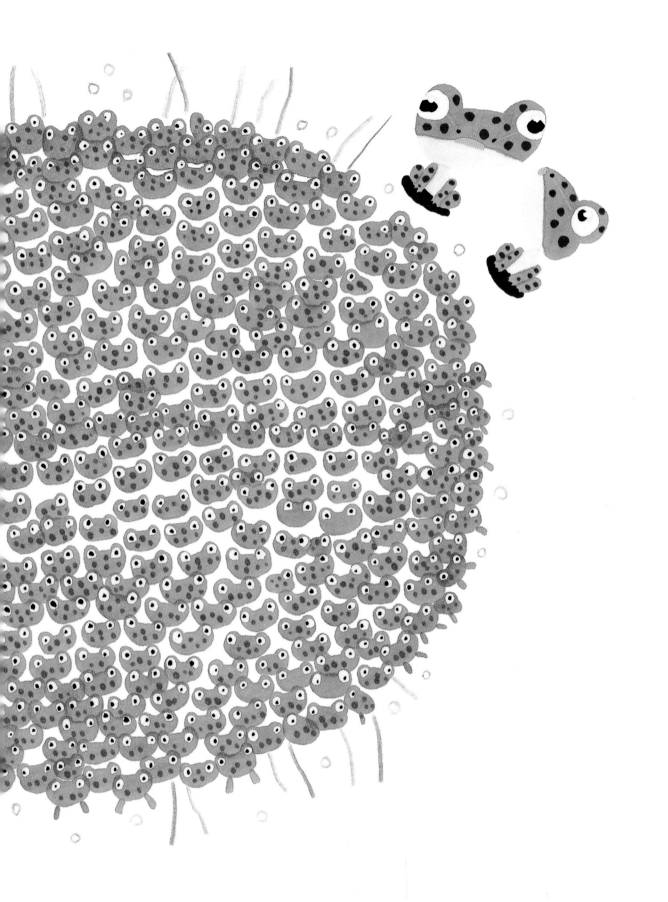

So 999 young frogs scrambled to get
out of the pond.

"SHHHH," said Mother. "The world is
a dangerous place. You must be careful."

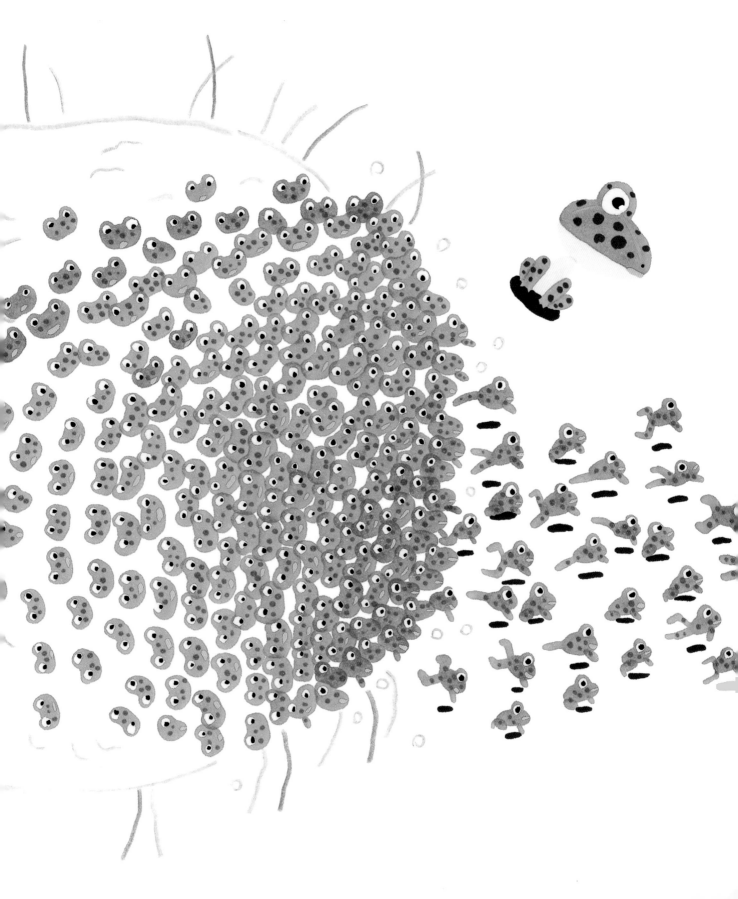

"Follow your father," said Mother.

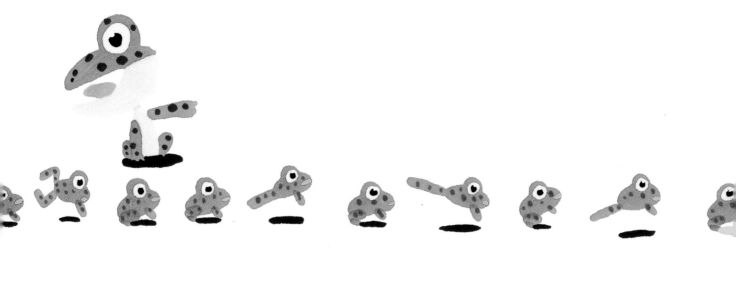

So 999 young frogs followed their father across the field. But no matter how far they went, all they saw was more grass.

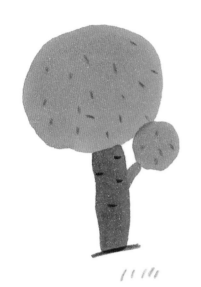

"When will we get there?" asked one.

"I'm hungry," said another.

"I'm tired," said a third.

"Keep hopping," said Father, "or a scary snake might get you!"

"What's a snake?" asked the frog children.

"A snake can eat a whole frog in just one swallow," said Father. "It has a very B I G mouth and a very LOOOOOOONG body."

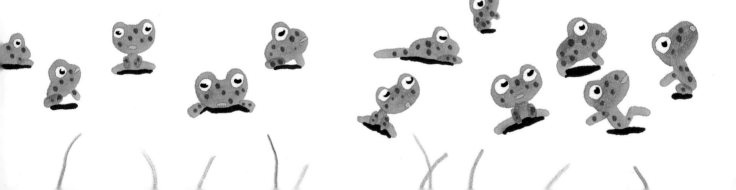

"Like THIS?" asked the children.

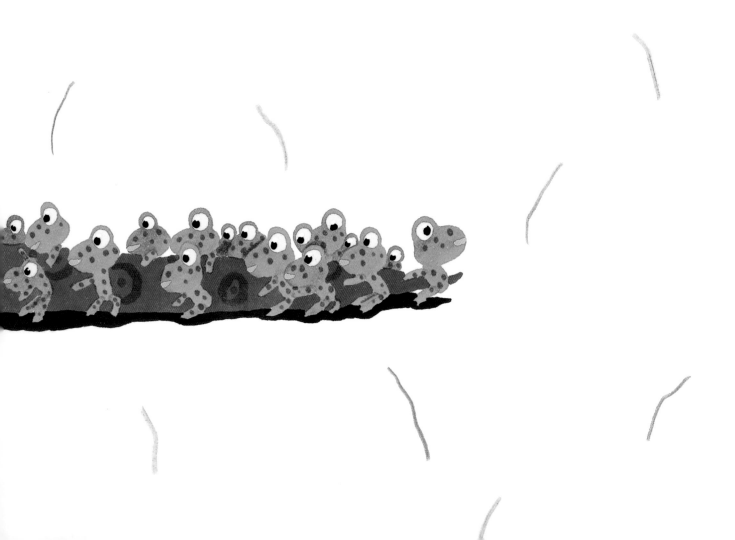

"YES!" said Father.

The snake was sleeping peacefully. It must have just eaten.

"RUN FOR YOUR LIVES!" said Mother. "Before the snake wakes up."

So 999 young frogs ran for their lives across the field.
They didn't notice a hungry hawk flying over their
heads. Then the hawk swooped down . . .

. . . and grabbed Father!
"LET ME GO!" cried Father.

"Not a chance," said the hawk,
and rose into the sky.

"LET HIM GO!" cried Mother, and she grabbed on to Father's leg.

"LET THEM GO!" cried 999 young frogs, and they grabbed on too.

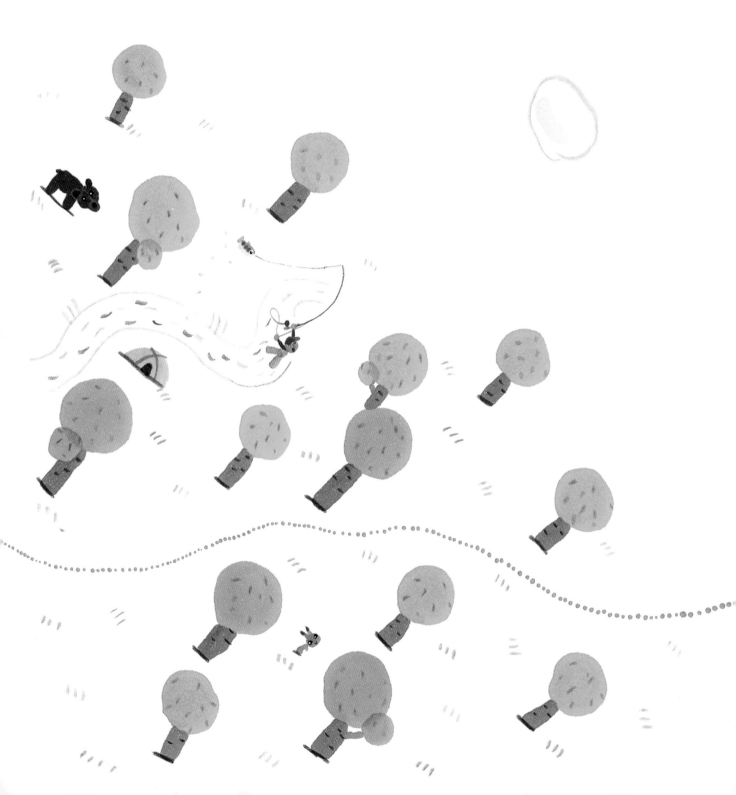

"Why is this frog getting so heavy?" the hawk wondered, and he looked back. Wow! He was carrying a whole year's supply of frogs! He was so pleased, he flew even higher.

The 999 young frogs loved it.

"This is great!" said one.

"What a view!" said another.

"Wheeeee!" said a third.

Mother and Father were not as enthusiastic.

They were worried about falling.

"Don't let go!" warned Mother.

"No matter what!" added Father.

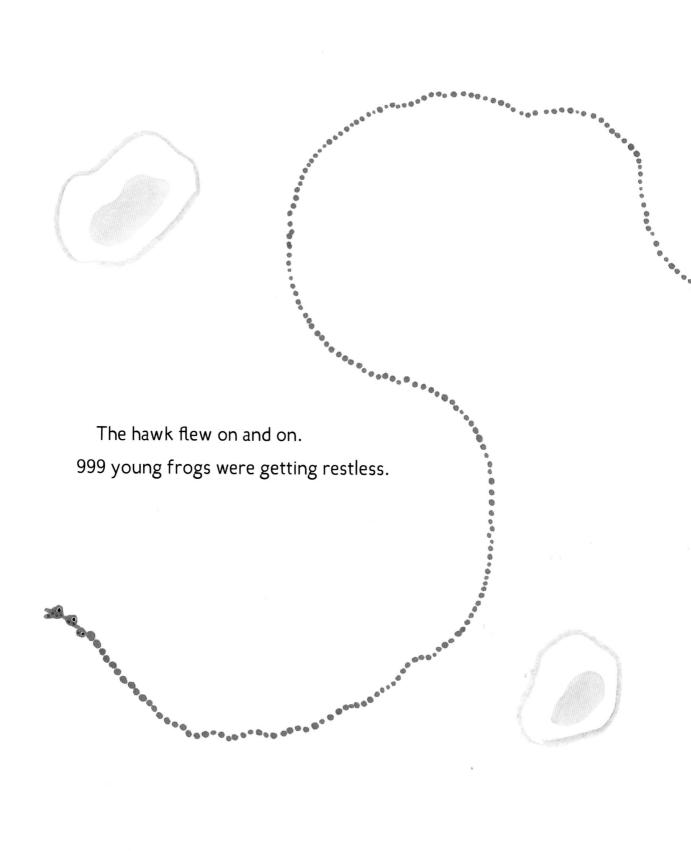

The hawk flew on and on.

999 young frogs were getting restless.

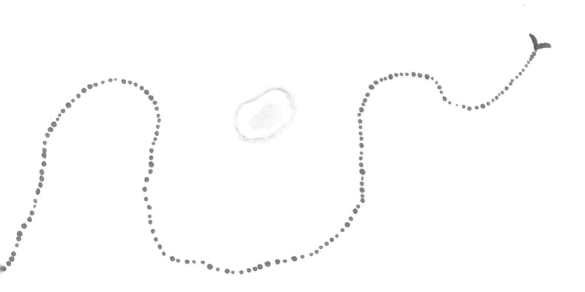

"I'm hungry," said one.

"When will we get there?" asked another.

"I'm tired," said a third.

The 999 young frogs began to wiggle. And every time one wiggled, the hawk swerved.

"Hang in there, Hawk," said Father. "Don't let us go!"

But the hawk couldn't hold on any longer.
"AAAAAAAGGGGGGHHHHHH!" Father cried.

Mother and Father and 999 young frogs
fell down from the sky.

SPLASH!

SPLASH!

SPLASH!

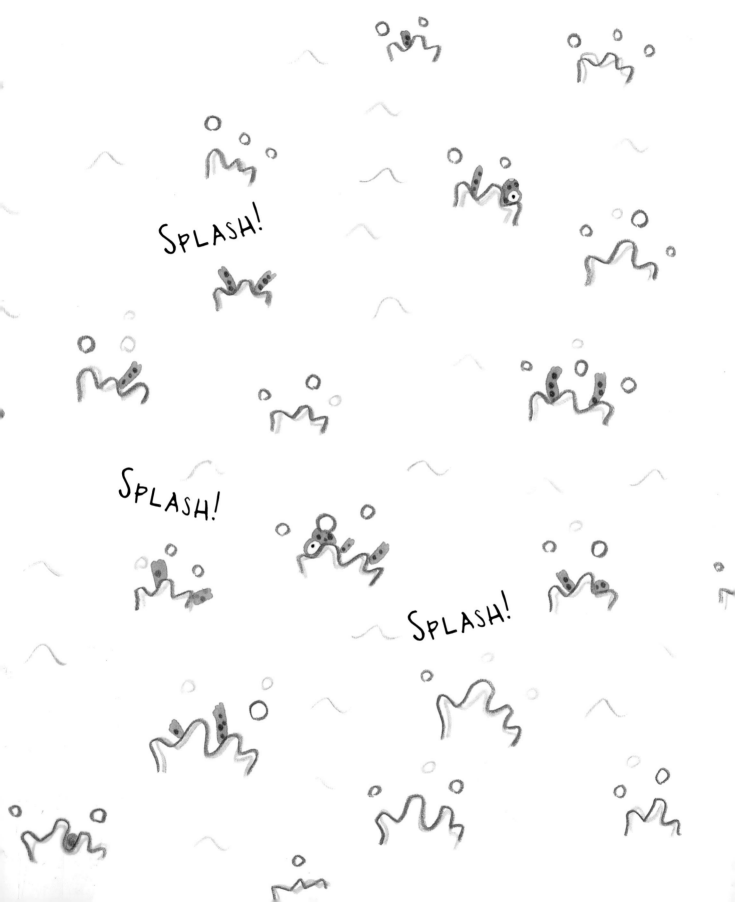

Mother and Father and 999
young frogs fell into a pond.
A **BIG** pond.

"It's cool!" said one.

"It's wet!" said another.

"It's home!" said a third.

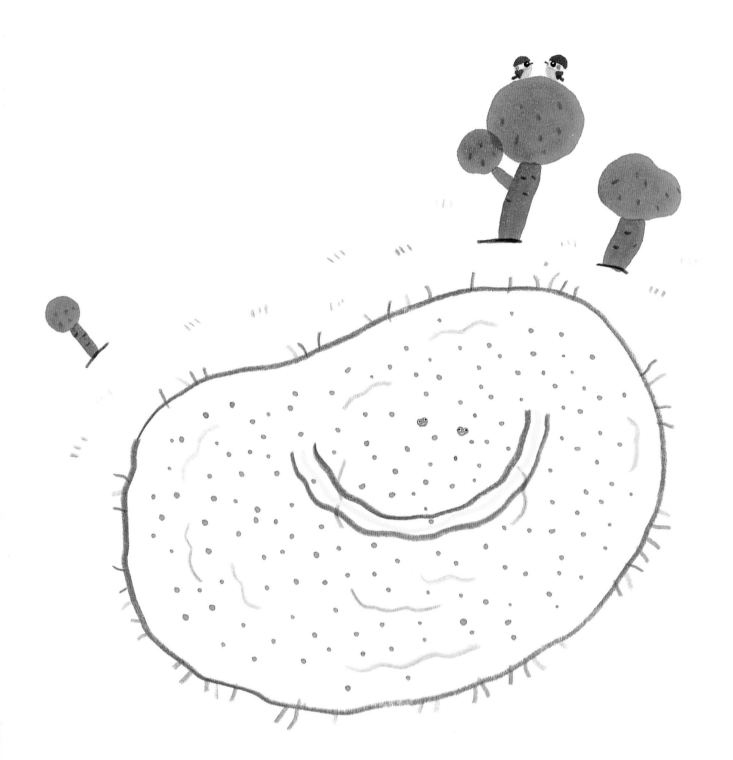

And that's how Mother and Father and
their 999 young frogs found a new home.
For all I know, they're still there singing

RIBBIT RIBBIT RIBBIT.